AJAKAVA

AJAKAVA

Chaitanya Murali

Space Wizard Science Fantasy
Raleigh, NC
www.spacewizardsciencefantasy.com

Cover art by MoorBooks
Editing by Heather Tracy
Book Layout © 2015 BookDesignTemplates.com

Ajakava/Chaitanya Murali.— 1st ed.
ISBN: 978-1-960247-12-4

For my grandmothers, Viji Paati and Baabi, my first and
fiercest fans. You are both sorely, sorely missed.

She came with the second flotilla of Felters, six years after the first had arrived on our shores. I watched them float into the dock with Amma, Appa, and Bhavani akka in the crowd beside me. We'd come into town to trade in our day's haul—four deer and some pockets full of rabbits. Then we got caught in the throng, the wave of flesh rushing from Vallarpattinam to meet its counterpart from the sea.

And the woman who stepped first from the lead ship was the one who had stolen my attention.

She was an older woman, black hair turning to white, weathered skin taut against her cheeks, like she'd seen the inside of one too many storms. But she carried herself with the careful, paranoid air of one who knew the woods, her eyes never settling on one spot for too long before flitting over to another potential danger.

The soldiers and guards of Felt Town were one thing, but now they were sending hunters over to our lands?

She scanned the crowd with eyes meant to blend with the forest—green as the light filtering through a rain-soaked canopy. And those eyes settled on me, narrowing, *hunting*. I broke contact, turned away from her and pushed out of the crowd, working on instinct alone.

She was dangerous.

"More of them keep coming," Bhavani akka said, later when we all sat cross-legged on the floor of our parents' home. "This group makes, what, five hundred Felters in their walled town? What happens when they run out of space?"

"We'll be long gone by the time that happens, so it's none of our concern," Appa said.

"What, just melt away into the forest again? What if we come out and there's none of us left? How long can we keep running from our enemies, Appa?" Bhavani asked. Rani, her partner, put a hand on her shoulder to calm her, but Bhavani shrugged it off.

"What would you have me do, Bhavani?" Appa asked. "You want us to drive out those five hundred ourselves?"

"You know what their gunships did to Nanganallur. We don't have the strength to fight that," Amma added.

Appa hesitated, and for good reason. We had seen what was left of Nanganallur after their "raid." Witnessed the craters where homes had stood, smelled the burned corpses of friends. They had left nothing standing there. And all the while, their two ships stayed a full kilometre from shore, beyond the range of sling or bow.

But Appa's chin stiffened, and he pressed on. "The forest is our home. It provides for us, and it protects us from those who would see us harmed. That is our way. We are not warriors, Bhavani, even as much as you want us to be."

"They've brought hunters with this group," I said, my voice cutting through the thread of conflict connecting Appa and Akka.

"What do you mean, Velu?" Akka recovered first.

"The old lady who got off the ship first. She had the eyes of a hunter."

Bhavani wheeled back to Appa.

"The forest is our haven, right?" She pointed at me. "What happens when they come for that too?"

"They won't. They fear it too much," he said.

"That fear will fade. It is already fading, if they are calling hunters over to this town. In time, they will come for the forests, take them the way they take everything."

Appa's words, when they came, carried the beat of tempered steel.

"Then they will learn that our forests do not take kindly to those who do not belong."

* * *

I dreamed that night of the docks, watching a woman set foot on our shores.

My vision was blurred from my deep slumber, and my twelve eyes could not focus closely on the frigate and the intruders it brought to my home.

But I felt it when her feet touched the ground, I felt the tremble run through the floor and up my legs, and from that, I knew what her coming brought.

I would rise from my slumber, wait at the door, pedipalps raised in anticipation.

It was time.

I woke enveloped in sweat, the voice from my dream still fresh, still resonating in my mind. And with it, the black pincers of a scorpion.

* * *

The forest is our home.

Appa's grandfather had been the one to break our family from the forester tribe, to have us make contact with the fishermen and weavers of Vallarpattinam. A point of contact, a means of re-entering society. He had wanted to know more of the world beyond the confines of the Katalkad forest that our tribe had called home for a millennium. The tribesmen took time to understand, to reconcile with one of their own who had seemingly turned his back on them, but they came around eventually—though they still only spoke to my family, avoiding Felters and non-foresters both.

So, we became the in-between, the ones living on the thresholds of two worlds, a perpetual twilight hour, caught between modernity and tradition. Expansion and the infinite confines of the familiar.

And that was where we situated ourselves.

Appa and Amma lived in a large wooden shack built outside the village's picket fence walls. They'd built it themselves there, cutting a swathe of woodland away to make a farm, far from the Felters and their machinations. They'd built a second house last year, for Akka to move into with Rani.

We kept ourselves distanced from Vallarpattinam and the Felt Town, preferring to stay where we had easy access to the woods. What we caught, we would bring into town each evening, one group going to Vallarpattinam, and the other paying the tithe to enter Felt Town. And the locals preferred it that way. They—even more than the Felters— didn't trust us. They had been born on the coast, staying near the water all their lives, never setting foot where they could no longer see the ocean, or feel its spray mist against their skin. To them, those of us who forsook the shelter of the water for the darkness of the woods were strange creatures, weird and perverted by that association, and never to be held closer than arm's length.

And that was why they took to the Felters so quickly, gave themselves over to them. They welcomed them into Vallarpattinam with garlands and rice, offered their homes to the newcomers until they built their own, and once Felt Town was built, they made the offer to serve the Felters, as soldiers, servants, cooks—anything they required. For if a people could hold such command over the ocean as they did, if the gods of the waves favored them so, then who were these mortals to distrust them?

The Felter gods, on the other hand, demanded that their faithful not be corrupted by other, false faiths, and so the first thing the original "settlers" did once they purchased Vallarpattinam from the nizam was to seal themselves away from us—taking the docks and the land surrounding it. They painted the walls and buildings of this town in the colours of their empire, white tinted black—the soot of their cotton mills, and the gunpowder residue on the sails of their warships. Then they built walls around this Felt Town and called it a fort—a defensive bulwark against their enemies.

It did not pass me unnoticed that our people were left on the outside of those walls.

And this evening, it was Bhavani and I who were tasked with selling our kills in the Town, so we paid the guards the ten paise we owed, donned the itchy and shapeless robes they required us to wear within their walls, and drove the bullock cart through into the wide, cobblestoned avenues of Felt Town. We drove past their temple and its preachers, past their barracks filled with guns and twitchy fingers, and out into their marketplace with its pale-skinned merchants glaring at us, at our impudence.

But the forests were alien to them and their kind, who had never seen trees grow to grab at the sun, who had never heard the cacophony of the night, the cicadas, frogs, nightingales, baboons and a thousand other voices joining in celebration of the dark; they had never been stabbed by the silence that fell in the advent of a predator, the singing replaced by a void where the only sound was the all-too-loud thumping of your heart.

And then there was the deep forest, close to the mountains sheltering us from the North. A fell place that even the most seasoned hunters avoided at all costs.

No, the Felters could not enter the forest without us.

And so, they tolerated Bhavani and me, even as they scowled at the mud our tracks left on their streets, the colour being all they despised.

I turned to the cart, breaking my gaze from the maze of gaudy clothes on sale elsewhere in the market, back to where a white-haired woman stood examining a buck I'd killed this morning.

The same one I'd seen on the ship. And in my dreams. Up close, she looked even more like a hunter, lean and wiry, with skin darkened by years spent under harsher suns than her homeland's. She turned from the buck to Akka and me, her gaze appraising. When she nodded, I felt a strange relief, as if I had just passed a particularly important test.

She spoke our language, accented and slightly broken, but better than any of the other Felters around. "I saw you at the docks, you still had your bows, so I guessed you were hunters. I'm glad to see I wasn't wrong."

She turned back to the buck. "This was a clean kill; the poor thing never even had a chance to realize it was dying."

"We try to kill them in one shot. That is the least we can do for the ones who sustain us," I responded.

"You want to buy that deer, Madam?" Bhavani asked, coming to my side.

"I want someone to take me through the forests here," she said.

"With all due respect, Madam, we aren't guides or bodyguards. Maybe you could ask one of your soldiers?" Bhavani said.

"Oh, soldiers are useless in there. I know, I've seen them floundering in woods a fraction of the size. I want you people, who understand what it means to be out in them." She smiled at us, and I felt the jaws close around my neck.

"I'm sorry, Madam, but do you actually want to *buy* anything?" I asked, and when she shook her head, I turned to hawk our wares at the house servants who scurried across the market.

I tried to ignore her eyes cutting into my neck.

She came to the market every day from then on, asking incessant questions about the forest and the creatures that lived in it. She wore us down through persistence and annoyance, comfortable in the knowledge that an outburst from any of us would only see us thrown from Felt Town. I broke first, when she asserted that the forest was too dense for large raptors to find success in them.

"Our eagles would shock you, if you believe that to be true," I replied.

And with that reply, she had her chance.

"Can you tell me what they look like? Are the females larger? What colours are they? How do they hunt? What do they hunt?"

I looked at Bhavani for help, but she had abandoned me, venturing further down the street so she wouldn't be caught in this problem.

"How can I make you stop bothering me?" I asked.

"You can take me through the forest. One time, and then I won't ask you for anything more," the woman replied.

"You're a hunter yourself. Why do you need me?" I asked.

"Only a fool ventures into foreign wilds without the aid of those who have lived those wilds for generations," she said, then added, "And I'm not a hunter. I'm a naturalist. My name is Eleanor Greyback."

One time. That was what her persistence had bought. But for all her inquisitiveness and her easy manner, I could not shake the fear I'd felt when she first spotted me in the crowd. Keep with her, and she would be my ruin.

* * *

I did as she asked and took her into the forest on my next hunt with Bhavani. She carried her own rations and water, along with a satchel stuffed with paper and charcoal. A naturalist, it seemed, did not hunt animals, but rather drew them, and collected notes on their habits. And so, Bhavani and I resigned ourselves to a day of waiting around as Lady Greyback sketched. She pointed animals out to us, and we explained what they were, then she drew them, muttering to herself the whole time.

Bhavani nudged me while Lady Greyback was preoccupied with a hummingbird. "You brought her here, so you watch her. I'm going to do our work."

She disappeared into a thicket of floating roots before I could protest, but then really, what could I say? She was right. Lady Greyback didn't mention her sudden absence, though she certainly noted it.

"How deep into this forest have you gone?" she asked.

"We stay close to the town, where there are fewer predators to compete with. The deeper you go, the wilder the forest becomes, its trees growing tangled and so thick they fall over you, closing you in. Only the foresters know how to traverse those depths. How to avoid the monsters that are said to live there."

I was trying to scare her, but she only seemed to grow more interested now.

"Foresters?"

"Tribes that live within the forest. Nomads who follow the ant carpets, taking up residence in the lands they scour, and moving when they sense the carpet's return."

She didn't know what an ant carpet was, so asked me to describe to her the most terrifying entity in the forest, the marching army that consumed any that dared stand before it, the natural calamity that cycled back each year to cleanse the forest of its rot. The beast that could not be slain.

And she wanted to see it.

I knew now why I thought her dangerous. Lady Eleanor Greyback was captivated by exploration, even at the expense of safety. Only fools would ask to see the ants.

Only fools and naturalists.

"I've seen horde behaviour in animals before," she said, rummaging in her satchel for a specific notebook and flipping it open to point at a page. "Banded mongooses, for instance, travel in packs of several hundred" — she turned the pages once more—"and there's another land, far from here, where thousands of zebroids and gnu march across the savannahs in a yearly cycle." The creatures she showed me were strange—the mongoose was smaller than the ones here, they could not possibly kill cobras; and of the other two, the first looked like a donkey which had been shoddily painted, while the other seemed like no more than a hairy, starveling cow.

They were fascinating.

We only caught two sambar deer that day, though Lady Greyback proved helpful in skinning them once we left the forest. As thanks for the tour, she bought both deer from us, and asked us to carry them to her house in the cart.

The guards at the Town gates flagged us but let us through without issue when they saw

Lady Greyback sitting up front. She took the reins from me there, and led the bulls down a side road, cobbled brown and white, towards the part of the docks the Felters had claimed. Her house, as it turned out, was a warehouse—one of several perfectly round sandstone buildings that workers had constructed to house the materials that went into Felt Town. Most had been torn down to make way for other, more necessary buildings once the town's foundations were set, but it seemed that this one had survived, a barnacle on the hull of the seafarers' jewel, and now found itself renovated for this woman's purposes. A sooty brick wall had been built around the hulking dome, encompassing its grounds and a smaller Felter building behind its iron gates.

No guards came to open the gate for us, so I had to get down and do it myself, pushing them screaming inwards and letting Lady Greyback guide the bulls inside.

"Would you like to come into the house?" She hopped from the cart and pulled a brass key from her satchel, its bow unfurling to either side of the shoulder in an expanse of gossamer wings. Keys—and locks—of the kind the Felters used were uncommon still, and entirely absent from our side of Vallarpattinam. An extravagance bought through paranoia, though not the kind I could empathize with. The Felters, it seemed, had a chronic aversion to trust.

"Us?" I asked.

"Where should we leave the meat?" Bhavani ignored the invitation and eyed the grounds, looking for a guard or someone to appear at the Felter woman's return.

Lady Greyback nodded at the other house inside the walls. "If you go around to the back, you'll find the servants' quarters. You can knock on the door and leave it there."

I wanted to follow Bhavani as she took the bulls that way, but a fascination took root in me, sealing my feet to the ground. Would there be more drawings inside? Other creatures she'd seen on her travels? Would they be as weird as the ones she'd shown me? She was strange, and dangerous, but Eleanor Greyback knew so much.

"You want to see?" she asked, the wings shimmering as she turned the key in the door, drawing me in as it swung open, consuming me. I was at her shoulder, peering into the darkness. She unhooked a whale-oil lamp from the wall just inside and lit it with some flint from her satchel. The death-light cast a cadaverous glow over her home, her workshop, illuminating shelves filled with the bottled ghosts of monsters.

Shelves of kaleidoscopic butterflies, their hypnotic wings spread in agony, warding away the one who had pinned them. Transparent bottles of liquid housing creatures just dead enough to seem alive—octopuses like the ones that sometimes clung onto trawlers' nets, angry at their meals being snatched; lizards with sail-like ridges that presently hung limply over their spines; parakeets caught mid-alarm warble—they were everywhere. A large desk sat in the center of all this carnage, plain and scarred, bearing the furrows of a mind frustrated. On it were open dozens of books like the few Eleanor had carried with her, as well as the inkwells and quills the Felters were fond of. And there Eleanor went, to sit with her captives staring down at her, cursing her with their voiceless accusations, and she was utterly unperturbed. She smiled at me, the death-light creeping over her table and chair and into the widening age lines on her face, shadowing the creatures all around her—a spectre of Death, hallowed by its light.

"Welcome to my lab," she said.

And the light enveloped me.

* * *

I began working for her the next day. A researcher, a guide, an apprentice. Bhavani protested, having seen Lady Greyback's collection herself a few moments after I did— she called it monstrous, a mockery of everything we did. The hunt was for sustenance, a task undertaken solely in the pursuit of life. It was not something to be used to collect the forest in pieces, as *toys* to display. There was a part of me that agreed with her, that rankled still at Eleanor's grotesque collection, but it was overshadowed by potential. By the chance to learn.

What Lady Greyback had that we didn't have was knowledge, a breadth of it that we couldn't match. And I wanted to know what she knew. See the forest the way she did. Not a hunter seeking a prize, expecting death; but an observer, a silent bystander watching the forest change around me. Through her, I could understand even the Katalkad and its infinite depths, perhaps even learn to recapture all that our ancestors had lost. Appa remembered little fragments of this—in the broken shards of the stories that were passed down to him. He had told us that our people had been scholars and engineers to put these invaders to shame, that they had traversed the lands and brought home knowledge beyond our comprehension. Treasures and powers that the world had only now begun to rediscover.

"Weapons and machinery had never been their way," he told us. "They lived within a forest and grew to understand it better than any others could. They devised methods by which to communicate with the woods, to get all living within it to join with them. Thatha even said they could command the forest to grow in certain manners—shape it to their liking, hiding them from those who would do them harm."

Our expulsion had set us back centuries, and instinct told me that working with Greyback would help me understand how a nation so wise could have been brought low. I would tell her what she wanted to know, show her the outer rim of the forest, and in return, I could learn the secrets of the deeper woods.

"This looks like the thagasu," I told her. I was looking at one of her drawings, showing a stocky beast with short legs and a fierce expression. It stood taller than the thagasu, but less broad. What confirmed my suspicions, however, was their eyes. Even through this illustration I could feel an unquenchable rage behind those beady black orbs. They were definitely related beasts.

"Thagasu?"

"It's like this one, but black with a white band running down its back. More vicious than anything else in the forest by far. If we smell its musk, we turn and go wide around that location. If we hear its rattle, we're already far too close." My nethers quivered nervously at the thought of the beast, which had a curious proclivity for attacking just that region.

She chuckled. "So, it's a relative of the wolverine then. Good to see they share traits even this widely dispersed."

"Where did you find this one?" I asked.

"Not far from Merino, our capital. It lives in...snow forests." She switched to her tongue for the word "snow," which was unfamiliar to me. She thought for a moment, picturing the words in her head. "It's water, but cold, colder than a mountain spring. You don't have a word for it, I think. Your lands are far too hot for it to ever form."

She showed me a sketch of mountains, like the Vindhyas beyond the far reaches of the Katalkad, but more jagged, more foreboding, lonely. Their peaks were white-tipped, early morning sunlight bouncing off them, splashes of blood on a deer's belly.

"That white part is snow, only imagine it on the ground, covering the earth like grass in a meadow."

I tried to picture it but couldn't. I didn't think she was lying, but I couldn't imagine this.

"What does it matter? I'll never see it anyway," I said, turning the page to another beast.

My breath caught, the continued complaints about snow dying in my brain, screaming their futility even as they were silenced by the image on the page.

It was a wolf, but it was not. The beast rose taller at the shoulder than the man Eleanor had drawn next to it for reference. Its eyes were burning embers of a forest fire, its claws scythes, and in its grinning rictus I could see a devilish pride behind slavering fangs.

"Ah, you've found them."

"Them?"

"The pages from thereon contain...flights of fancy. My hobby."

Wasn't naturalism her hobby? Most of the Felters here seemed to have come simply for the novelty of the place.

She saw the question in my face but didn't take badly to it.

"You saw me for a hunter when I landed here," she said, "and you took these butterflies and bottled lizards to be my prey?"

I needed water. I felt cotton mouthed, my tongue fighting its way swollen to the back of my teeth.

"I come for the animals, but I *stay* for the legends."

She pointed to the wolf on the page in front of me. "That one's a giant wolf that was said to have terrorized a town in the days before Merino unified the Felter fiefdoms. It was hunted by an army and fled into a bottomless well to escape them. The well was bolted shut, with rocks piled over it to suffocate the beast. But three days after its capture, a guard out for a morning piss found the well destroyed, the rocks scattered across the fields around it— pad marks in the ground, ringed with burned grass leading away from the site, into the woods. He fled to report the beast's escape, but try as they might, none could find it again."

She turned through the pages, each fascinating and terrible in equal measure. "This one is an elephant said to have six tusks, and to be white as marble. This one a jackal that ferries the souls of the dead. This one is a crocodile so large it pretends to be a bridge across rivers, only to roll when its hapless victims are on its back, drowning them."

She showed me more, but the images and words melded together in my mind, a mismatched beast of nightmare that called to me, sang to me of its allure even as teeth gnashed behind its human head.

"You...you hunted these?" I asked, looking around the room for evidence of one of these monsters, unconvinced that a person could have slain one.

"Good heavens, no! I want to *find* them. What all these pictures have in common is that they are drawn from my imagination.

Renderings born of stories I have heard on my travels."

"Is there one here?" The hunter flared to life within my chest, the hummingbird thumping of my heart calming to the steady pulse of a cat in the tall grass. If a beast like these existed here, what would it be? Could something be in the Katalkad? In the ruins of our ancestors?

"That's what I want your help with." Eleanor said.

Anyone else would dismiss the idea for madness, a product of childhood terrors. But Eleanor would consider it, or more—she'd believe it outright.

I opened my mouth, thought the words, but couldn't summon them to my lips. Despite my curiosity, despite her interests, she was still a Felter.

I'd search for them myself.

"I don't know anything," I said instead, but she only shook her head, leaning closer, hawk eyes cutting into my lie.

"Stories, myths, anything they tell children to keep them in line?" she pressed.

"Nothing I can remember." I shook my head. She frowned, likely thinking of ways to look into my head for herself.

"What about the foresters? Would they know anything?"

I shouldn't have told her about them.

"They keep to themselves; we don't really know much of their ways." The words caught in my throat for a moment. Her eyes narrowed, finding the lie, readying to dive in for the kill.

"You don't want to tell me."

"I don't know anything, really," I stammered, though we both knew that wasn't true.

"It's fine. I can't imagine I'd want to share my family's secrets with a stranger if I were in your position, either.

"I'm not going to force it from you. I've made that mistake before, and it nearly cost me everything." She pulled her baggy shirt up, turning to show me her side, where a large rosette of scar tissue blossomed near her chest.

"My first expedition was so very nearly my last. I was young, stupid. I thought too much of myself, my station. I coerced my guide in that land, threatened him with death, or worse, should he refuse to give me what I wanted. Threats born of the pedestal my skin gave me. A pedestal of shifting sand, that fell away beneath me when I made the smallest misstep.

"In the middle of the forest, he took me away on false pretexts; said he'd found a hidden path. And then, when we 'chanced' upon a boar and her young, he pushed me into them; left me to be gored to death."

She pulled her shirt back down, showing little hint of the embarrassment most of her people felt at the sight of bare skin.

"How did you survive?"

"Luck, nothing more. The boar missed my lung and heart, and I got a lucky shot in with a pistol. I managed to drag myself back to my camp, and still nearly died. Suffice to say, I don't deal in threatening those whose stories I want to find anymore."

"So, what do you do now?"

"I wait. You can tell me whatever it is when you're ready to. When you trust me."

She smiled, an easy expression designed to calm.

I think back on this, and see it now for the feral grin of the tiger that hides in the grass. Confident, implacable, conniving. Endlessly malicious.

* * *

I stand alone in the center of an amphitheatre, my audience an overgrowth of vines and weeds. Parasites, come to live off my performance.

Something moves in the thickets of spectators at the back, a different beast, one more discerning than the rest of them.

"Do you know where you stand?" Its voice pierces my brain, laps at the runny material within my skull.

"Do you know whose bones you crush into dust beneath your feet?"

A thousand scuttling feet drown the whisper of my audience's whistles, shushing the leaves, holding their breath captive. And they thin, curling away from the force that speaks, revealing the slightest glimpse of the world beyond my stage. I see a palace. A mausoleum. A wonder of brownstone, garlanded with the decay of time.

And under it, glinting the reflection of the light shining on me, are eyes.

Unblinking. Unwavering.

Twelve eyes of solid black, a raging inferno burning in each.

And a segmented tail that rises high above those eyes, ending in a curved spike that promises unendurable pain.

Her gaze pierces me, penetrating into the deepest part of my soul, and discards me as a finished meal. A body spent, with nothing valuable left to offer it.

Even her admonishment carries a wicked humor to it, as if toying with me. I am not worth her anger, not worth her retribution.

In the presence of this ageless, timeless creature, I am meaningless.

I know this looking into her alien eyes, feel the truth of it echo within me.

Her questions, and this city she brings to my mind, spark that longing I'd felt within me at Appa's tale of a time long lost to us. What must those days have been like, when humans walked with such a beast? When we had possessed the strength and knowledge to rival any in the world? She is right to shame me for having forgotten the old ways—because I cannot fathom the majesty of her. I should feel chagrined, chastened.

And yet, I stand before her, and am in awe.

Fear should rule me, but all I feel is elation.

Until that tail stabs down into me.

* * *

Around us, the town thronged, swarmed like a hive stirred into action. Disturbed by danger. The agitation passed from one to another until Vallarpattinam and Felt Town both bustled with nervous action. Impatient.

A pigeon had come in, bearing the seals of those distant kings beyond the Vindhyas, whose subjects we nominally were. The Felters had been granted this land by zamindars and local lords, but officially, Vallarpattinam belonged to the kings beyond the mountains, who had never once looked in our direction.

But with our overseers growing in power and confidence here, they had been forced to turn our way, to give us the grace of their condescension.

This was a summons. Official recognition. Vindication for the Felters who chose this remote outcropping of rock for their new home. A chance for them to put the second part of their plan into motion.

They scrambled now to prepare a caravan, and a platoon of guards, to send through the forest and the mountains beyond, into the wider nation so far inaccessible to them. As Bhavani and I took our usual spot in the market, we could see Felter guards loading up the seven bullock carts they'd judged a reasonable sum to present to a king, filling them with bolted chests of unknowable treasures from somewhere across the seas.

"They've asked Guna and her family to be their hunters for the trip, to make sure they don't run out of provisions," Bhavani said.

My gut unclenched in sudden relief. Had I been afraid they'd ask us?

"How are they going to get through the forest?" I asked.

"Guna says they're sending over fifty soldiers with them, so they want to push their way through with brute force. Straight line to the Kambavi Valley in the Vindhyas."

She grimaced. So, she thought it a bad idea too. The forest was ancient. It demanded respect. Not the bumbling charge of armoured soldiers crushing it underfoot. But there was nothing we could do. Whatever became of this group, it was not our concern.

Three figures stopped in front of our cart, and I began asking what they'd like before I saw the brown skin of their hands and the quivers at their hips.

"Not a bad haul, Velu," Ravi said. Next to him, Valli and Muthu stood watching the caravan being readied. They carried no kills.

"No luck for you today?" I asked.

"Scouting, not hunting," Ravi replied.

"How far did you go?" Bhavani asked.

"Beyond the nadhi, Akka. Past the opposite shore, to the edge of where the light reaches."

"Tomorrow, we go deeper, and then even deeper each day until this damned caravan leaves," Valli said, eyes still fixed on the Felters beyond us.

"It's eerie. I threw a torch into the darkness today, still couldn't see more than five paces ahead of it," Muthu said.

The three were my friends from childhood and fellow hunters in Vallarpattinam. I knew better than to tell them to stay safe in the forest. They knew what they were doing.

"We only have to clear the path to the forester village. Guna's the one who has the rough task," Ravi said. "It's not that bad for us."

Still, his fingers drummed on the cart stand, sending tremors of unease through the wood and into my heart.

"What brings you into the Town?" Bhavani asked. "You never come here."

"Delivering scouting reports to the guy leading the caravan—some Felter lieutenant."

"That one, over there—with the bushy orange face worm. Bellamy, his name is." Valli pointed at a man who was barking at some labourers who had just dropped a heavy chest while lifting it onto a cart. The chest was undamaged, but the Felter was incensed at the boys. We could hear the wet slaps of his riding crop on their backs from across the courtyard.

"Seems a pleasant enough man," I said.

"Vaaiya moodu," Valli grumbled.

"Speaking of pleasant Felters," Muthu said, "How's your work with that kezhavi?"

"She's not that old, you know," I replied.

"He brings her along on every third hunt, is how it's going," Bhavani said. "She's such a pain, always sitting and drawing things and slowing us down. And Andava, the questions!

She just never shuts up!" She pulled at her hair, only exaggerating her frustration the tiniest amount. On two separate occasions I'd had to talk her out of using Eleanor as bait. Akka really wasn't fond of her.

"Most of the animals we have here are new to her, apparently, so she's always trying to learn more about them," I said. "She can get in the way of hunts, though."

"I've asked him to stop bringing her, but he's infatuated with her. Won't stop talking about the drawings she shows him in that creepy house of hers."

"I'm not infatuated with her. I just find her *interesting*. She has notes upon notes on how every beast's body works—what each muscle does, what the *purpose* of every part is. Have we ever thought of them as anything beyond food or offerings or potions?"

"Why do we need to?" Bhavani countered. "We've gotten by without that information for so long, why is it necessary now?"

"She has a point," Ravi said. "We know what parts to use, and what to cut out and throw away. What else do we need?"

He then turned to pay close attention to the caravan when I glared at him.

I couldn't make them understand that I wanted to understand *why* creatures were the way that they were. Look at them beyond base need. Understand how they came to be.

And I couldn't tell them what Eleanor had shown me in her books. What haunted the corners of my mind.

I couldn't tell my sister of the things I saw in my dreams. The eyes that had watched me in that theatre every night for these past six months, that taunted me for forgetting. The skittering steps that seemed to come from all around me, holding me captive within the amphitheatre, prisoner to that voice.

"Ah, he's done whipping those kids." Ravi tapped the table with his knuckles, drawing me away from the vision.

"Means it's our turn to deal with the thevadiya punde," Valli said.

Muthu lagged behind them a moment.

"Can I come with you to her house sometime?" he asked, quietly, trying to keep the question from Bhavani though she was glaring right at him.

I nodded enthusiastically. Anything to make them see what I saw in Lady Greyback's work. Anything to have someone to talk to about the thing I saw.

"Get lost, Muthu. Don't encourage him." Bhavani brandished a sheathed carving knife, shooing Muthu away from us. With him fleeing, she turned the blade onto me. "And you, don't go getting others to sympathize with that woman. Bad enough that you're doing it."

"Why do you hate her so much?"

"Instinct, thambi. You're ignoring what yours told you the first time you saw that woman. Her people might be crass, but they're open in their derision. Disdain is trustworthy. It's predictable. The Felters will always choose themselves over us, but they don't hide that.

That woman shows interest in us in the open, she says all the right things, but inside, she's no different than the rest of her kind. She's hiding something. And trust me when I say that nothing good will come of her friendship."

She put the knife down, leaned hard on the cart-stand, eliciting a groaned moo from two sleeping bulls.

"I don't want you to learn that when it's too late."

* * *

I've seen this dream before. The same amphitheatre, with its sandstone steps, and me at its heart. The silhouette of a palace in the distance, its minarets snapped, its domed roof falling into itself. I've seen it almost every night now for six months. I hear the sharp-metal sound of her legs striking flagstone, just out of sight, as always.

Always in the back of my mind, always in the corner of my eyes. A presence that seems attached to me, weighing me down all my waking hours, then taunting me in my dreams.

I have given up trying to communicate with her. She does not respond, and none of the other creatures here—the ones I occasionally hear crying from somewhere beyond my confines—ever venture into the amphitheatre.

When I have tried to leave my prison, I heard hissing emanate from the darkness around me, a warning not to go beyond my bounds. I remember the sting from the first dream, and the very real pain it caused me the next day, and I obey. If she can draw me here in my dreams, and if she can cause me physical harm *in* a dream, there is no telling what other control she can have over me, and I do not intend to find out.

And so, there is nothing to do here, except wait.

And I get the sense that she too waits for something. And when that time comes, I will be brought to judge.

I sit down in the dirt and settle until that event comes to pass.

* * *

"They're going to die," Eleanor said, nonchalant, unconcerned.

I had gone to help her with finding insects for her collection, guiding her through the woods in the morning, and was now setting up the insects for preservation in the manner she had shown me when she spoke.

She was sketching again, something new that she wouldn't yet reveal to me—not until it was done.

"Who?" But there could only be one subject to comment on.

"Most of them will die on the journey. And even if some make it through the forest and past the Vindhya mountains to give their tributes to whatever kings they find beyond, I doubt they'll make the trip back."

The charcoal scratched against paper. A claw scraping stone. Mandibles grating. Twelve eyes red, blazing in the darkness of a ruin.

"What are you drawing?" I asked.

"Our wise president knows this, of course. He sends them to pave the way, the same thing we've done in every land we've conquered."

They mean to invade.

The thought was not mine.

The darkness peeled back, revealing legs carved from stone, rising to an onyx carapace, tail curving to a wicked spike.

She pushed her chair back, its wooden legs screeching in pain. The page was in front of me now, the scorpion staring into me. It was a messy drawing, the lines blurring between where the scorpion began and the shadows ended. A drawing born of fear, of nights spent scanning the edge of the bed for those eyes.

"You've seen her too," she said.

"I...I don't know what she is."

"She knows us, but..."

She pulled her chair aside and beckoned me closer to the desk. The world around us had gone quiet in the night, and the darkness around her death-light seemed to flicker as I approached, each blink bringing the darkness closer, until my world had reduced to nothing but her, the light, and the page she had open in front of me.

At the depiction of Death itself.

"Tell me," she breathed, "what do you know of the name Ajakava? The name Vijayam?"

The name birthed the ghost of a memory in my head, a story told by the light of a campfire deep within the forest. A story meant to remind us that the wilds were beyond our reckoning, beyond our power to control.

A forester story. A fractured remnant of an ancient past. A story I could not tell her.

I felt cold, an alien tongue crawling over my back. Arachnid feet skittering on my skin. A pincer poised at my throat, leaking gleaming droplets of venom.

"You know something."

A pause, death-light flickering on the scorpion-god.

"You cannot tell me."

I shook my head.

She slumped in her chair, fiddled with the raised corner of the page in front of her. For the first time in the time I'd known her, Eleanor Greyback seemed...frightened.

"What does she tell you, in the dreams? Where does she take you?"

I felt the sliver of betrayal, a shiv cutting into my side, but the torment of Ajakava's visits outweighed that guilt, forced my mouth open.

"She takes me to an amphitheatre, long abandoned by humans. And from the borders of the pavilion, she watches me, talks to me. Tells me I have forgotten who I am, forgotten my way. Every night she takes me there, berates me, keeps me awake and watching for her every move. But since the first night, she has never come forward to me, never revealed herself in full to me. She always stays just beyond my vision and urges me to search for what I have lost. To go deeper into the forest. To reclaim my past."

The words left me empty, hollowed for a moment before relief swept in their vacuum. A relief tinged with panic, a realization that in speaking the words, I had made it real. No longer just dreams, but woven into fabric, tied loosely around my neck. But that relief brought with it a sense of loss, a dull pain that filled me, that begged for closure. An acknowledgment that the creature was right. We were shadows of what we had been, nomads who stole from the forest that had once bent to our will. Who recoiled from its heart, where once we had made a home. There was more the god had told me, which I could not yet bring myself to tell Eleanor. Hints of an ancient wrong that the god wished to set right. A wound that despite the years, had only grown wider and turned to rot.

She, I sensed, needed me to save her. As much as I needed her to sate my thirst for a home. We were kindred souls, split across time.

Eleanor watched me through eyes ringed with fatigue, sunken into tired flesh. But there was a spark there now, a renewed hope.

And that, more than the spectre of a bestial god, terrified me.

"She calls you to the forest?" she asked, the words a whisper of unspoken thoughts. "Calls you to her?"

"What do you see?" I asked, a chill running down my spine at her tone.

"Warnings. Flashes of rampages past. Threats that I know better than to give voice to amongst my people.

"They believe me mad already, if I went to them with ravings about giant monsters coming from the forest to kill them, they'd string me up for a witch," she said, chuckling dryly at her predicament.

"You think they'd know better by now, with what I've shown them in the past. With the knowledge I've brought to light in the lands they've taken. For following through on folklore and myth, unraveling threads in culture that helped foster their relations with the ones they sought to usurp. You'd think they would grant me some modicum of respect for it all. But it's never enough for them. What I do is lost in the face of industry—buried beneath an influx of cotton and coal. I—we—can never do enough to make ourselves known, Velu. But that's fine. This...Ajakava...is far beyond anything my people have encountered, and I will not tell them of her until I have studied her myself."

She stopped, chest heaving with the sudden, violent force of her outburst. Her hand gripped the edge of her desk, tightening as if she wanted nothing more than for it to rip free in her grasp.

Then she calmed, knuckles grew pink around the table once more, and she steadied.

"No, they will learn once I am ready, once my preparations are in place." She focused on me again, her eyes glinting like arrows in flight. "All in due time."

A promise.

A threat.

Behind her, the scorpion's eyes blazed in the light of the whale oil.

* * *

You have not forgotten me entirely, then.

I am at the lip of the amphitheatre this time, looking out into a part of the forest I had never seen before. The darkness had retreated, revealing to me a valley nestled deep in a corner of the Katalkad, directly under the peaks of the Vindhyas.

I stare into the ruins of a city; into roads, their flagstones broken by time, riddled with creepers; into circular houses of sandstone turning slowly to dust, flaking at the brush of my fingers, their leafy occupants curling away from me in abject terror.

This is what remains of those who opposed me.

I look for Ajakava, but the scorpion is hidden from me, her scraping voice coming from everywhere and nowhere.

And their descendants do not even remember the terror of my name.

Her voice quivers, furious.

And sad?

"What do you want from me?" I ask. The first response I gave the creature, the first acknowledgement of her abductions.

For you to remember what you have lost.

Ajakava's voice fades, and she responds to none of my cries.

Spurred on by her disappointment, I venture further into the ruins, weaving through streets that still bore the remnants of its people's hurried exit—a discarded toy horse grown over with the roots of a balsam; a clay pan still lying on its kiln, though the food its owner had been making was replaced with the bloom of a bromeliad that had mistaken the kiln for a tree. Their homes still stand in parts, stone and clay foundations holding firm against both time and the encroaching forest, and they are nothing like the thatch huts we use now—for ease of reconstruction after coastal storms. No, these are solid structures that would withstand those storms and shrug them off with little effort.

They look almost like Felt Town.

The city falls away abruptly just beyond two slowly decaying walls, sloping down into two aqueducts, divided almost into rectangles—and presently home to thousands of nesting mosquitos and several massive lily pads. A groove cut into the bottom of the aqueduct had once sent water into the greater city via a central canal, but its mouth is blocked now by a rockfall that had taken place at some point over the years.

What is this place? There are no such cities near Vallarpattinam, and nothing we knew of beyond the Vindhyas spoke of a lost city either. The kingdom there was new, only a few centuries old, and this ruin speaks to a history far older than that.

I spy animals—deer, foxes, a pack of wild dogs—at the edges of my vision, but they stay far from this strange beast that had ventured into their world. I wonder how I appear to them. Am I the spectre haunting their home? A visitation from their onetime hunters, their ghost of bedtime terror?

I do not blame them for their fear.

The streets of the lost city begin to converge into a square, a central gathering spot. The trees part at its mouth, in solemn memory of the royalty that had walked that path, the canopy lifting to bring into view a palace—its exquisite shikhara rising above the crumbling walls of its once-mighty fortifications.

Come find me.

Ajakava's voice rings out from within the palace walls, a slithering toll that drives a cloud of birds to screaming flight.

An invitation from the devil.

* * *

The Felter envoy left three days later in a gaudy procession that hinted at the funereal. We said our goodbyes to Guna, and she feigned excitement at being a pathfinder, at breaking new ground—no one from our town had ever made this journey by land before, given the perils of the Katalkad and the snow-covered peaks beyond it. We knew, though, that her excitement was little more than a front, as we all felt the same dread settle over us. Somewhere within us, I think we knew that she would not return.

Lady Greyback did not come to see her people off.

* * *

One month is how long they estimated it would take for the convoy to reach the capital beyond the mountains, but three months after they departed, a second bird arrived from the North bearing a letter stating that none had come from the forest.

The Felters turned their suspicions upon those of us who knew the forest best; friends of the Felters who'd gone on the journey accosted hunters, insinuating that Guna had turned the convoy off its path in the forest, or worse, had led them deliberately to their deaths. "Where had the rest of us vanished during the days following the convoy's departure?" they asked, as if we had not returned to the village each and every day to sell the furs and meats of our forages. In their eyes, we had conspired with Guna to kill their envoys and make away with the myriad riches they had sent. No matter that none of us bore any sign of that wealth, or that we still sold our wares to them at rates far lower than we would like, for fear of their wrath.

With one tragedy, their demeanor changed. No longer were they peaceful settlers living by that lie of joint profit—now they watched us with the eyes of the hunted, the bared fangs of the cornered. More guards patrolled the walls of Felt Town, their knuckles white against the barrels of their rifles, fingers trembling just off the triggers.

They closed the gates to Felt Town earlier and earlier, letting no one but those of white skin to pass through once the sun began to set. And even the townsfolk were not spared the Felters' paranoia. Those who worked as servants—or otherwise were in close contact with the Felters—were dismissed, and found it hard to find other employment within those walls.

But us—the ones who split our lives between the town and the place that had swallowed their friends—we were scorned.

We were the in-between, the ones whose allegiances were a mystery; the ones who could not be trusted.

* * *

Bhavani akka, Valli, Ravi, Muthu and I took what we could from Guna's home—her spare bows and their strings and the tapestries she'd woven depicting her hunts—and transported them into the forest at night. We carried only the light of the moon with us, but this was a familiar path we treaded, a dirt road paved by the feet of those who remembered, heavy with the weight of their loss.

We waded through clusters of bougainvillea and rubber, under the gazes of knowing owls, the barking of mandrills echoing our grief as we carried the last of Guna on our heads.

The path was clear, maintained by foresters, who used it far more often than our meagre number did. Seldom did one of ours fall within the forest.

When we reached the death-grove by the river, the elders among the hunters were already waiting, their skin cut above the spine to add three new notches, three more dead to carry on their backs. Appa and Amma were there too, holding garlands of malli and marigold and nitya to drape on Guna's things what should have gone on her body.

We laid "her" down on her bier, our parents having done the same for her family, and stepped away to give the elders room. The smell of incense rose in the wet air, driving back the clouds of mosquitoes that paid no heed to the ceremony. They lit the sticks all around the bier and sat cross-legged before it, their hands clasped in silent prayer.

The foresters sang their prayers, but they were not hunters. Theirs was not a life devoted to silence, where the slightest sound was the difference between life and death. We revered silence, and only in that vacuum could our grief be cast in its fullest.

When they finished, they rose as one and moved away, and our parents took their spots, lifting the biers atop their shoulders and carrying them into the waters of the nadhi, setting them soft to float into the dark of the deep forest.

They were home.

* * *

"When was the last time Ajakava reached out to you?"

Eleanor looked more tired by the day, the bags under her eyes growing darker, giving the impression of a displeased raccoon. She'd been sleeping poorly since the scorpion's first visitation, I knew, but since the news of the convoy's disappearance she seemed not to be sleeping at all.

Instead, she spent all her time at her desk, sketching maddening images of ruin that I picked up and hid every day, lest someone else wander in and take her for a witch.

The latest one, the one on her desk presently, was a now-familiar sight. Eleanor, grey hair flying wild around her face, stood watching from the stern of a Felter frigate as an army of darkness roiled beneath her, its waves pouring through Vallarpattinam and over the walls of Felt Town—what were once called impregnable. The rest of the fleet, the Town's pride, burned in its harbour, its cannons useless against these invaders.

And in the back, shrouded within the forest, eyes of glistening ruby watched Eleanor.

"She shows me more. Visions of what will come to pass if I do not heed her call, now that my people have encroached on her forest."

"When did you last sleep, Ms. Greyback?"

"I asked you a question first."

I sighed.

"Just before the convoy left."

"Why? Why does she show us different things? What is she looking for?"

"I don't know, but you must try to get some sleep." I tried to coax her from the chair, but she slapped my hand away and pulled open the book that held her notes on all things mythical.

"What did she show you last? What does she want from you?"

"It showed me the town beyond the amphitheatre, all grown over with plants. The remnants of some lost peoples."

"Why you?"

"I don't know."

"That's a lie. I've given you a year, Velu. A year in which I have shown you everything I have learned. Is that not enough for me to earn this little sliver of knowledge from you?" She looked at me with tired eyes, the accusation sharp within them. *Tell me, and I might be able to sleep again.*

I felt Akka's disapproval like nettle-rash on my neck.

"We're descended from foresters—most of the hunters—so that is our home. Maybe she shows us different things because I belong to the forest, and you do not."

But she was already shaking her head.

"There's more to it than that, what does she *want* from you?"

"I don't know."

Come find me.

Giant wrought-iron gates hung precariously on rusted hinges, wind whistling through the arrow slits cut into gilded murals beaten plain by time.

She saw the realization on my face. Fatigue turned to a greed so visceral it almost dripped from her mouth.

"What is it?"

"I think she's calling to me."

She sat upright, claw-like fingers scraping at wood for charcoal and paper.

"Where?"

"A ruin, deep within the forest. An ancient fortress. The home of her foes from a bygone time." Unease pricked at me as I responded, wariness tinging my words a lilting suspicion.

"Vijayam."

The word was a ghost, a phantom caress against my cheek that left me chilled.

"Can you find this ruin?"

I shook my head. "I have never seen them before, never heard tale of them."

"Will the foresters know?" She pressed, insistent, *ravenous.*

She means to answer the call.

I felt my sister's heart break when I buckled under Eleanor's gaze, when my head tilted in concession.

I felt my heart soar, the burden of this quest lifted from my shoulders, at the responsibility, the blame, the fault being passed over to the easy target.

The deep forest, its mysteries and its demons—I would be the one to find them. *I* was the one chosen to find them. But its logistics? The anger that would come with this expedition? Those were Eleanor's to bear.

Eleanor did not seem as one burdened. Her jaw was set in resolve, her mind already working through the logistics of searching for this beast that haunted our dreams.

Our delirium was shattered by the sudden coming of light, the sharp footsteps of an angry man. The door to Eleanor's workshop had been thrown open, and a man was approaching us, his eyes bloodshot under a sweat-soaked wig.

"Get out," he said, without pausing to glance at me. "I have business with the Lady."

Eleanor said nothing, but the man's tone had troubled her.

I made for the door, turned from their sight, hid the shame that blossomed in my face and ears.

"President Dartmouth, to what do I owe the pleasure?" Eleanor asked.

President. *That* was the Felters' leader?

His response was whispered—too faint for me to catch—but his tone was urgent, frustrated. Eleanor matched it, and I could do nothing but wait outside the door like a good little servant until they were done.

Dartmouth left quickly, the meeting lasting less than five minutes before he stormed back out, nearly walking into me. I scrambled to move out of his path, but he continued on as if there had never been anything there—as if I was invisible to him.

I peered into Eleanor's workshop, and found her bent over the table, her nails digging into the wood.

"How soon can we leave?" she asked.

"Give me some time to find out more about it," I replied. There were questions I had for her: What was Vijayam? What was she seeking there? What did the president want from her?

But I couldn't give voice to them now. Now, I just wanted to get away, to be able to breathe again.

I left feeling small, a spider amongst the Felters—useful for one task, but fit only for disgust outside of that. A creature to be crushed underfoot if it ever stepped out of line.

Eleanor didn't care about us. I don't think it had occurred to her that Ajakava might have killed everyone in the convoy.

An hour later, I stood at the threshold of my home, Narasimha's breath heavy on my throat as I crossed it. A pulpy wetness, a sudden rash of sweat on my throat cold as spring water brought me back to Earth. I'd have to tell Appa and Amma of my betrayal. Akka...she'd see it on my face the moment she saw me.

The vision of the castle prodded at my mind once more, a throbbing reminder at my temples. She was waiting. And all I needed to do to prove my worth was to find it.

They sat cross-legged on jute-woven mats, banana leaves spread open before them in anticipation of Amma's food. Already the line of accompaniments crowded the edges of their leaves—maangai oorga, aviyal, thoran, vetha kozambhu, and pepper chicken—armies set to march on the rice and rasam that would be placed at the leaves' hearts.

Appa, Rani, and Bhavani akka turned their gazes from the kitchen, its roaring flame, and the smell of the spiced crab rasam above it, to look at me. Lately, they'd ignore my entrance and wait until I changed and joined them for dinner—knowing that to acknowledge me at the door was to acknowledge what I did, and that was the one thing they would not give me.

So, I went to them.

I washed my hands and feet with the clay paanai and ladle just inside the door, then sat before them, demanding their attention—disapproving or not.

"Appa, where did the foresters come from?" I asked.

"What did you do?" Akka realized first, her fist crushing the spine of her leaf.

"*Who* did we come from, before the forest?" I asked.

Amma came in then, pouring steaming rice onto their leaves and following it with ladles full of rasam for them to mix into the rice. Fourth and fifth leaves appeared as if from nowhere to be placed before and opposite me. When she'd filled these last two, Amma took her seat, a cue for us to begin eating. The argument died unspoken, and for a time the only sounds to be heard were those of chewing.

After, Appa went to the back of the house, setting cow dung on fire and letting the smoke drive the mosquitoes and the damp evening chill away. Then he called for his children to join him under the stars, settling us onto the ground while he placed a pot of chai over the flame.

Clay cups were passed out as we waited for him to talk, our breaths held so close that the wisping curls of steam rising from the tea moved not an inch as it passed our faces. Appa liked his stories, cherished them, measured their tellings with the stingy eye of the dam-maker. Heritage, he maintained, was something to be passed down over one's lifetime—a wealth of knowledge only appreciated if meted out in sparse doses, best remembered if the telling spanned decades.

But Bhavani couldn't let him begin without getting her word in.

"Appa, he's told that vellakaari something. You don't have to give him more of our secrets to spill to her."

"Velu, why do you ask of our ancestors now?" Appa asked. "When you, and your sister, believe the heart of the forest to be in our past, and to be ours nevermore?"

"I don't believe that. I *want* to know what's deeper in the forest. That's why the vellakaari interests me. Akka wants the forest to be our hunting grounds, and nothing more. You want us to remain here, at the edge of civilization—with the parts of the forest we know as a fallback. I want to know what we lost to the forest. What empire fell that tainted the woods around it with its death throes."

"Empire?" Bhavani asked.

"What do you know?" Appa asked, his voice steady, but undercut with tension; ripples in the chai moments before it comes to boil.

"I see things when I sleep. A city in the forest." There was no hiding this from them now, I'd prepared myself for their scorn, for Akka's dismissal of my worries. But Appa, he'd have an answer, I hoped. Anything, no matter how dissatisfactory.

"It lies abandoned, as if left in a hurry. There are still remnants there, overgrown with weeds as they are."

Appa's face was a demon's behind the fire.

"And does something call to you?"

"She's real, then?" Bhavani asked. Appa nodded, his eyes never leaving mine.

"Does a creature call you—bid you enter?"

I wanted to deny it, wanted to hide the truth of Ajakava from him. If he knew, he would never allow us to set foot within the forest again. But when my mouth opened, I could only answer in the affirmative.

His reaction was not one of fear, or of distress. In that moment, Appa's expression resembled nothing so much as Eleanor's when I told her of the city—a hunger that seemed to hollow flesh, consume them until there was nothing left but that burning need.

A hunter starved.

"Appa?" I ventured, unnerved by his gaze.

"It comes once more, then," he whispered, unto himself, his children forgotten. His eyes turned to the stars, to Anusham, Kettai, and

Mulam—their forms conjoined to become an arachnid, dark and vast in the night sky.

Bhavani nudged me, confused and concerned. I shook my head; what came now was what I wanted to learn.

"This was knowledge I only learned from your thatha on his deathbed. An ancient history only known to the oldest of the foresters. If thatha hadn't chosen to leave the forest, I would only have received this story when I reached my seventh decade."

"What is it?" Bhavani sounded equal parts worried, irritated, and reverential now.

"Our people did not always call the forest our home. Ages ago, hundreds, thousands of years ago, we had an empire far greater than the one that sold us to the Felters. This town's name even comes from that empire, though it knows not its roots."

Amma and Rani had joined us now to sit, bask in the glow of Appa's storytelling.

"Its borders stretched beyond the mountains, claimed with a steady fist all land it came across. And its rulers governed from here, within the Katalkad—their capital, Vijayam, hidden from all, nestled where the forest meets the mountain, hidden behind a curtain of ice-water."

He pointed to the scorpion in the sky.

"A being of wisdom and strength, a revenant of the forest, was approached by the kings of this empire, and they begged her guard their borders, act as their second

line of defence. Ajakava was her name. A scorpion, timeless and unfathomable. In return, they promised not to eat into her forests.

"Through centuries she watched them blossom, prosper under her watchful eyes, until her heart was opened to a new emotion—a human emotion—by one who she had caught trying to sneak into Vijayam.

"'Wait!' the man cried, while Ajakava held him in one immense pincer. 'Why do you serve them, when you are far greater than they?' he asked. 'Why do you slave for a land that gives you nothing for your generosity? That takes from you, from what they promised never to touch?'

"His pleas bought him a moment, and the man spilled everything he knew from the previous times he had snuck into Vijayam. He was a poacher and a smuggler, one of many employed by the empire to hunt the beasts under Ajakava's protection in the forest—in order to feed the ever-growing number of mouths to feed within its lands. And on the other side of the capital, where Ajakava seldom went, Vijayam had begun to expand its borders, pushing into the Katalkad's sister forest and tearing down trees that had stood for millennia. Soon, he promised, they would turn to her.

"Ajakava was perturbed. She sat to think about this once she had eaten the man, dwelling on the thought long into the

winter, when the waterfall she guarded had turned solid, and when her own carapace began to crack under the pressure of her constantly growing body. But it persisted, and when the summer came, she molted once more, discarding the green brown of ages past for a carapace of black and red, to reflect the anger she had reached in her conclusion. The humans of the empire of Vallaram, the king and queen of the grand city of Vijayam: they owed Ajakava reparations. Penance for the years they had used her and stolen from her. A renewed promise that their expansion would not break the terms of their agreement with her.

"The rulers, in their arrogance, rejected the scorpion's demand. A mighty nation owed nothing to anything—least of all a beast. Ajakava did not take kindly to this. She retreated from view, forwent her defence of the city, and settled to plan. The forest outside of Vijayam grew dark, tangled with the newfound malice of its guardian spirit.

"People began to go missing, one by one. Those who went hunting found nothing of the lost, and some were lost themselves. A rot had set in the kingdom's heart, trapping its citizens within. But they could wait it out, they had the stores to outlast any inclement condition. The gates were barred, a curfew was set. No one was to leave

Vijayam's walls. The forest was no longer their home.

"They waited two years for their armies, for any sign of aid from the rest of their vast lands. But none came. Whether Ajakava repelled them, or whether the world believed Vijayam lost—no aid was forthcoming. The city despaired, and asked its rulers to return to Ajakava, to seek forgiveness. To give the god what it rightfully deserved."

The wind had picked up now, whipping the fire into a frenzy and brushing embers against our faces, but we were too engrossed to pay it more heed than hissed curses.

An unease pricked at me during his tale—the god I had spoken to sounded little like the vain monster he painted—but I shook it away as Appa continued, his greying hair fluttering against the nape of his neck as he watched the scorpion in the sky.

"But it was too late. The king and queen sought out the scorpion bearing gifts, asking for amnesty, and of their entourage only one returned to the city—their son and heir, Ram. He was bloodied and poisoned, but even in the throes of his fevers, his eyes burned with rage.

"When he was fit once more, Ram descended upon the forest with axe and torch, slaying what he saw, and burning what he did not. The air reeked of roasting flesh, and thousands of Ajakava's spawn *fell from the flames to curl and die before Ram. With his act, the city's demise was confirmed. His army had foregone its defence, and those who remained within its walls fled, taking what they could and running far from the cataclysm that was approaching.*

"For three years the remaining children of Vijayam fought against the children of Ajakava, slaughtering one another until naught remained but the charred husks of a once-great people. The rotting carcass of a verdant mystery. And the unquenchable hate that bonded man to scorpion.

"When the last of their lines fell, only two remained—Ram and Ajakava themselves. The pair had fought on countless occasions through the war, seeking each other out at every opportunity; and now, they would finish this. Their fight took them through what was left of the forest, until Ram was driven back into his ancestral home, into the throne room of his parents, in whose memory he fought. And there, he cast down the scorpion, driving his axe through the god-monster's armoured exoskeleton and into her blackened heart. But he no longer had the strength to pull his blade out, to finish the job. And there, together, the bringers of ruin fell."

He let the words float on the wind, carried with smoke to die within the forest they belonged to.

"But you said it comes once more," Bhavani said, breaking the silence. "Which one comes?"

"Ajakava," I whispered.

Appa's eyes did not leave the stars, but I saw the lines around them ripple, a wave of muted rage spreading from them to his cheeks, driving a fevered flush into them.

"Her heart was pierced, but she is still a god. Ram did not have the strength to finish his task, and so that must fall to us—his descendants."

"How can we defeat a god?" Bhavani asked.

"We do what we have always done. We hunt."

* * *

"What does Greyback know?" Bhavani asked, as we applied beeswax to our bowstrings the next morning.

"You've told her about the dreams?" Amma added, more intrigued than surprised.

"She's been having them too. Since the convoy went out."

"Ajakava found you two because you've been thinking about monsters?" Bhavani asked.

"Ajakava found them because she was *looking*," Amma said. "Searching for memories scattered by time."

I'd told them what Eleanor wanted from our land—I'd had to, once they knew of my visions. Along with everything else, and with Appa's backing of my story, it hadn't been hard to convince them of Eleanor's goals.

Bhavani already thought her mad enough for it.

"She sensed kindred spirits," Amma said, smiling. "Muttaal pasange."

They shared a laugh, and I peered into the town, hoping to catch a glimpse of Appa returning. Without him, they'd just tease me to no end. Drive me right into the forest to answer Ajakava's summons out of embarrassment.

Appa, when he did return, brought with him a number of familiar faces—my friends, their expressions stony.

"We know the deep forest better than you," Valli said without preamble. "If you're going in there, we should lead you."

Amma and Bhavani glared at Appa, who met my eyes instead.

"They have a right to this hunt, as much as you do," he said.

"What do you know?" I asked them.

Appa hadn't told them much. I spent the entirety of our foraging that day—ranging up to the jagged edges of the deep forest mangroves—filling them in. When we returned, past mid-afternoon, they joined Bhavani and me on the cart to Felt Town. When I got off to set the stall up, they pushed me aside—Muthu and Ravi joining Akka— while Valli blocked me off, tree trunk arms crossed over her chest.

"Go get her."

"What?"

"This woman's the reason this creature is calling out to you. She could be the reason Guna's *dead.* If we're going to hunt the scorpion down because she did something, I want to talk to her first."

Her tone could have sliced mountains in half.

I left immediately, cutting through the market and between the neat rows of large wood-and-brick bungalows the Felters had built. Imitations of their homeland, spreading from lands like a fungus—a pox across the skin.

I turned a corner, out of my friends' sight, and directly into a pair of Felters, armed in the manner of their "privateers."

Pirates, we knew them to be.

"Oi, where do you think you're going?" one of them asked, as two bayonets lowered in front of me, barring my passage. His friend grinned, teeth filed to points, menacing and wild.

"Cut the mongrel some slack, Rob, he probably can't read the signs."

"We should teach 'im, then, shouldn't we, Fred? Do our duty, be good Samaritans and all that?"

I lowered my head, kept my eyes on the floor.

They'd been itching for a fight since the caravan's disappearance. I didn't need to give it to them.

Don't give them any chance to hurt you.

Bide your time. The hunt is about patience.

Hunt?

"I am visiting a friend who lives near the Felt Docks. She asked me to come by to help with an experiment," I said, careful to keep the growl out of my throat.

"An experiment," the one called Fred said, questioning.

"We don't like experimenting with your kind, savage," his friend added.

Your eyes roving over bare skin in the sun, ever so guilty, say different.

I did not rise to the bait.

"Lady Eleanor is expecting me—I have been her guide and apprentice for the past year," I replied.

"Oh, *you're* the savage she took on? Her new bait," Rob said.

"Oh, that's him? Poor bastard, he's got it worse than if he *was* 'experimenting' with her," Fred said, grinning.

"What's your name, kid?" the first guard asked.

"Velamuthu. I've just been showing Lady Greyback the wilds, the beasts and plants that you don't get in your homeland."

"I didn't ask what you do. Answer the questions and offer no more," Rob said, pushing me in the chest.

"So, the Huntress has you showing her the forest, huh?" Fred asked.

"That's how it always starts, isn't it?" Rob said. "She *just* wants to learn about the savage lands, nothing else."

I stayed silent. Eleanor had already told me of one of her early mistakes, and I could only assume there had been others she'd made. I'd heard a few rumours, Felters whispering to one another when Eleanor and I left the Town to go to the woods. "Huntress," they called her, even as they shied away from her laconic gaze—skittish deer, ready to flee the tiger in their midst.

"She meddles with things best left alone, and it's always others who die because of it," the one called Rob said, his tone rougher now.

"Keep helping her, boy, and you'll learn that for yourself—when her hunts find their way back to the ones you love," Fred said.

"What do we care if he dies? I just don't want her dragging ours in again," Rob said. "Like that bastard Dartmouth with his gods-damned expedition." He spat, not far from my feet.

"Wasn't his fault they got lost," Fred said. "They knew what they were signing up for. Equal risk, but equal profit from the venture."

Some realization passed between them, a spark of violence spreading sudden understanding, and they eyed me—taking in the muscles of my arms, and the scars there that weren't fully hidden by the shapeless monastery tunic I'd been forced to wear at the Felt Town gates.

"You're one of those hunters, aren't you?" Rob asked, orange moustache shuddering with rage.

"Please, I only want to speak with her. I have no quarrel with you," I said.

"Quarrel?" he said, voice low and dripping with venom. "You woods-loving bastards got our friends killed! I'd say you've got more than a quarrel with us." Steel flashed, a well-maintained sword singing free of its scabbard at his hip. I took one step back, the man following, only for his friend to drag him back.

"Not here," Fred hissed. "We'd never hear the end of it from Dartmouth and his lawyers."

The other one shook his arm free and pointed the sword at me.

"What did you do to them, you fuck? Drive them into a river? Hunt them down like game? Tell me, so I can do ten times worse to you." His voice was deathly calm, the sword held steady in his hand. "Everywhere we go, you savages are the same. Pretending to be servile, pretending to be happy for our embrace, and then the first fucking chance you get, you hide in the shadows like the cowards you are and ambush us." His words were angry, a fount of frustration picking at the cracks in his mind until it broke through—but his eyes, his eyes were *tired*. They carried the weight of countless horrors seen, countless campaigns like this one, and they bore the anger of his thoughts, the depravity of his words, with the fatigue of lifetimes.

I bit my tongue, tasted the iron in my mouth. I shouldn't react. I *couldn't* react.

I took a step away from them, back towards the marketplace. I hoped my friends were still at the stall, that *anyone* was around who could keep these pirates away from me.

"Rob, it's too open," Fred whispered, pawing at his incensed friend.

"What do you think you're doing?"

Her voice came as a blessing, sending a lightness through legs tensed for flight.

Eleanor hurried down from the Dock gates to stand between the guards and me. Ink stains had spread themselves over her like the plague, staining her burgundy coat and dyeing parts of her hair black. She carried rolls of canvas and paper under her arm, that now hung precariously in her grasp as she faced down my attackers.

Disgust oozed down the pirate-guards' faces, contorting and twisting them into something unrecognizable, something alien.

And there with it—flowing viscous and thick from their brows—was fear. Fred pulled his friend away, the latter aiming one last wad of spit at me before they fled wordlessly into the safety of their town.

I didn't feel relief at their retreat. I didn't feel grateful to Eleanor, I didn't feel sad or upset at the accusations. I felt suffocated, the white-and-black walls closing around me, visions of Felter nooses—linen cutting into my neck—crowding my mind, with me swinging at the end of each.

Never again would this town feel safe. Never again would I find anything resembling peace while these people remained in our land.

I was leaning against a wall, a hand—calloused, rough—holding me up as my knees threatened to buckle. Eleanor said something, but the words were filtered by the wall growing around me, a web sealing me in with my fear.

I was breathing hard, lungs straining to burst through my chest, heart pumping until the only sound left in the world was that of blood roaring in my ears. I was on the ground now, back pressed against a wall for support, hands wrapped around my knees.

You fear death?

A voice, a thousand chitinous voices, cut through the web, through the panic. I held onto it like a man drowning.

This was not death.

It hummed, a screech of multitudinous pincers grinding against each other.

It was not. What was it?

The word came, as if it had always been there, a seedling of discontent that had grown with each moment I spent inside Felt Town. That had fed on their fury since the expedition.

Desecration.

The humming grew, content, loud, overwhelming. It calmed me. Drove the panic from my heart.

Good.

Twelve eyes of red watched from the recesses of my mind, then blinked out of existence.

Come to me.

When the fog of panic cleared, I was staring into the tired, but concerned eyes of Eleanor Greyback, her papers resting carefully on the ground as she kneeled in front of me. We were still in the same alleyway, just out of sight of the market.

She relaxed when I came to my senses, sighing in relief.

"I was just about to call for help," she said. "Are you okay?"

I nodded, my jaw too sore to speak.

"That was battle-shock. It happens to those who've faced death, sometimes."

You're wrong.

"But you've faced death countless times in the forest, why would this affect you so?"

It wasn't a question directed at me, I realized. Her interest was academic—even were my jaw not sore, she wouldn't have cared for my explanation.

She's no different than the others.

My eyes strayed to her papers, their edges unraveling to reveal sketches of the forest, the branches of its trees twisted to form the outline of a scorpion.

Where was she going?

"Velu, are you okay now?" she asked.

I nodded, working the stiffness out of my jaw, pushing myself shakily to my feet.

"Are you going somewhere?" I croaked.

She grabbed up the papers, rolling them into an unruly bundle and stuffing them back under her arm.

"I was returning, actually," she said. "I saw you just as I was turning into the docks."

"From where?"

"I was meeting the town president, to request an expedition into the forest."

"For Ajakava?" I asked.

"She's been calling to me, showing me visions of what will come to pass if I don't seek her out," she said, words born of fervent belief. Maddened prayer.

"How did he agree to another one? Everyone's already furious."

"Dartmouth, unlike many of the idiots he brought with him, recognizes the importance of my research, the benefits it can bring to Merino. Especially in the wake of an ill-advised, ill-planned disaster." She sounded smug.

"What will you do if you find her?"

But this question had her confused.

"Talk with it, *learn* from it," she said, as if that was the most obvious thing in the world.

"And the people you take with you? What will they do?"

She waved her hand in my face.

"They won't know. For them, it'll be a punitive mission against the forest, with an appropriate target for their anger. The scorpion and the lost kingdom are our secrets."

The shadow of guilt prodded at me, its touch weak, fading. I didn't owe her solidarity in this. They weren't her stories, her gods, to find.

She can't have Ajakava.

"But you have to understand," she was saying, "the president forbade my using any natives on this expedition. I'm sure you know better than anyone why."

Behind her façade of sympathy, I felt the presence of something else.

Greed.

She really is no different than the others.

"But this is yours as much as is it mine, so if you'd like—would you take a scouting party ahead, make the way clear? You'll be the first to the ruins. The first to see it."

We'd be the ones killed by whatever dangers lay in wait, while her people climbed on our corpses to reach their goal.

But we belonged. The forest would not take us that easily, she would find.

"We were planning the same thing, actually. I was coming to discuss just that with you," I told her.

"Wonderful! Then it's settled, your group will leave a day ahead of ours, and we'll follow on your path. Easy and clean."

I did not take her back with me. When I could, I wobbled away from her, and let her return to her planning.

I went back to my friends and told them of the new expedition. The new obstacle in our path to kill the returned god.

Their path.

Eleanor's sketch came to mind—the nightmare that prompted her plan.

Not just a threat.

A portent.

* * *

The Felter warband was assembled over the next two days—a force of grumbling, miserable soldiers more accustomed to choppy waters than to the mocking laughter of the forest. But this group, unlike the previous, was outfitted for war. They carried axes, torches, and globes of some strange liquid that burned on contact with air, a last resort, should the forest bar their path.

This was an expedition that sought revenge, that wanted to bring the world to its knees. A force seeking to cow nature into submission—or let it perish and wade through the ashes left behind.

"They will die," Appa said, turning away from the procession of soldiers milling around the Felt Gate. That summary dismissal was all he had said about Eleanor's expedition since I told him of it. Three words, and no more. They merited nothing more for their crime.

We were to lead by two days—a group of seven hunters: Appa, Amma, Akka, and myself, along with Valli, Muthu, and Ravi. A smaller group, and more mobile. Their pace would never match ours, so we'd have ample time to find Ajakava before they could reach us—if they reached us. Best to keep them far behind us, with their plodding trek attracting Ajakava's—and other beasts'—attention. Appa didn't want to be anywhere near them, and to be in and out of the demon's lair before the Felters ever arrived, if indeed they did.

We found the first body at the river at the close of light on our first day—on our side of the water, with the dark Katalkad grinning at us from beyond, at its first gift to us. Puckered welts rose on dozens of locations on the man's body, which had been stripped bare of clothing and armour. The body was pale, drained of blood. Near it, we found the squelched corpses of black leeches, grown fat and long as my arm.

They had left early. And worse, they weren't following our path. What was Eleanor playing at?

"He must have fallen in when they crossed upstream. Can't be more than six hours behind us, if they reached the river there already. Pulled himself out here, but the leeches got to him before he could tear them off," Valli said.

"Bigger than the leeches I'm used to," I said.

"Get used to it."

She walked to the edge of the water and dipped one boot-clad foot in. The water frothed around it from the thrashing of dozens of tiny bodies burrowing at the leather. When she pulled her foot out, a few seconds later, it was black with their bodies, each trying to drag its way over the boot and onto her calf.

We slept a good distance away from the water that night.

Three hours before dawn, we awoke, and Ravi took out mud gourds filled with tobacco oil, which we spread over ourselves liberally before stepping into the water. The leeches still came for us, but they balked at the taste of tobacco, fleeing back into the safety of the river's depths.

We paused on the other side for a moment, taking one final look at the lands we knew, that we were comfortable with, before the three who had made this journey before, who knew its horrors, set foot into the nightmare once more. I glanced at Bhavani, seeing my nervousness echoed on her face, then we followed.

The forest changed. This was no longer the Katalkad. There was no way it could be the same forest anymore. The trees, the bushes, even the air was different here. Webs covered the upper canopy, creating a maze of white that the sun's rays struggled to pierce through. That, and the river near us, created a damp that pervaded the area, turning tree bark to mush under our hands, and the grass underfoot to treacherous slopes that led down and into an underbrush of thorny vines, looking like nothing as much as jagged teeth.

This forest was not home.

It didn't take us long to find the first scorpions. Normal-sized ones, running on the forest carpet, in tandem with centipedes and recluse spiders. Dangerous beasts, but they paid us no mind, running between our legs and back into the wilderness around us.

No, it wasn't them, deadly as they were, that worried us. The canopy above us creaked with the movements of bodies much heavier than finger-long spiders. We had passed into the realm of monsters. For now, we kept moving, staying close together to present ourselves as too much trouble to hunt. We broke our march only to eat quickly, shoving dried meat down our throats as fast as we could and foraging for what edible fruits we saw.

The second night, we slept in pairs, with three groups keeping watch in different directions. Nothing attacked, but everything watched us. They knew we were here—and they knew we didn't belong.

We saw the occasional deer and other prey animals, same as in our forest, but somehow...more fierce. Their horns grew more jagged, the velvet ripping from them in streams like arterial blood; tusks breaking through lower lips to curve up in front of their mouths. They showed no fear of us, not even when we shot them, they only looked to the skies in disdainful appeal—as if something was to drop down and save them.

We saw no predators.

When we woke the next morning, we found our clearing surrounded by these beasts. Warm-blooded like us, but ancient and feral, watching us with eyes that remembered an age-old foe—deer, bucks pawing at the ground; rabbits with jagged horns rising from their heads; rodents large as pigs; buffaloes with antlers wreathed in foliage—they all watched us with unbridled hostility, willing us to leave.

But they did not attack, no. They opened a pathway amongst them for us to follow, where the skittering shadows in the canopy grew thickest above us. We watched the skies for hints of them, and they soon made themselves visible to us, as the other animals backed away. Thousands of glassy eyes watching our every move, reporting them back to a demon awakened from a millennia-long slumber. Giant arachnids, each large enough to eat a gibbon, skittering in the trees and making no effort to hide their presence from us—that was behavior reserved for their prey. Us they watched intently, but without any intent to attack.

They veered west of us, creating chittering archways for us to pass under, shepherded onto a makeshift road by obsidian mandibles promising a painful death. We crunched our way through a carpet of bone, from creatures ranging from mice to elephants—nothing seemed beyond the reach of these apex predators.

Which begged the question: why limit themselves to this side of the river? Why would they not cross?

They guarded something.

We spoke little amongst ourselves, but held to one another, forming a chain beginning with me and ending with Muthu. Best to keep us all on our feet. These monsters might be tolerating us for now, treating us like some exotic spectacle, but I didn't want to find out what they'd do if one of us fell.

"Do you think *they'll* get this treatment too?" Bhavani whispered to me.

"Eleanor was seeing visions too, right? Maybe it's a test?" I replied.

"See who breaks first and attacks the bugs?"

"See who doesn't."

"Where are they taking us?" Muthu asked.

"Feeding ground, probably. Herding us like damn sheep," Ravi said.

"This doesn't feel like they're herding us," Appa said. "More like...an escort?"

"Taking us to meet their queen," I said.

"And what happens when they learn we're here to kill their queen?" Valli asked, in the barest of whispers.

They were everywhere, hundreds of inscrutable faces bearing eight eyes each, one for each leg. They watched us with an intelligence beyond the animal, conduits to some ancient hivemind.

The path they formed for us ended with the treeline, opening into the entrance to a cave system, mountain bedrock dotted with hive-like caves. I saw a portion of the rock wall shift and pull away inside, briefly revealing the spider holding its makeshift door in its mandibles. Our guides stooped to enter that doorway, giving us little time to think of our next steps.

The last paused at the door, all eight eyes trained on us.

"We have to follow it," I said, but Bhavani tugged at my arm, holding me in place.

"We go in there, we die," she said.

The spider entered the cave, leaving us to our discussion. Plainly, they did not care what we chose now.

"We should go back," Bhavani continued. "We know they're here now; we can tell everyone, prepare if this demon chooses to attack. Seven of us can't kill a thousand of those things."

"I don't think we could kill one," Ravi added.

"We could," Valli said, "but it's not worth dying here for."

"Aiyya, what are you doing?" Muthu asked, breaking off the argument.

Appa and Amma had moved to the center of the clearing and were setting up camp.

"They don't intend to kill us, so it's best we spend the night here. Rest, and then decide in the morning," Appa said.

"You want to stay here? Those monsters could very well be what killed the last caravan!" Valli exclaimed.

"And if they wanted us dead, we would be. I'm not going to tempt them to change their mind by going back into the forest at night," Amma replied. She was determined, a vision of our ancestors who knew these woods.

There was no retort to that. Only a sullen resignation to the wisdom of elders.

* * *

I woke up to the sound of a scuffle and rose in time to see Ravi and Appa—the last watch—being overpowered by a dozen heavily armed soldiers. The rest of the Felter party burst through the undergrowth, surrounding us before we could pick up arms. They kept coming, more than the dozen I'd seen—more than twice that number, and still it didn't stop. But for all their numbers, the Felters had been worn down by the forest. They looked tired and dirty—covered either in blood or mud or both.

Eleanor came last, the crowd of soldiers parting to let her stand before us—her captives. My condemnations died on my tongue.

There was nothing in her eyes suggesting familiarity. Nothing to show for the year we had spent searching together. Staring down at me, she saw nothing more than an insect.

No different.

"She's beyond that cave, isn't she?" she asked, her tone icy, demanding.

We didn't respond.

She turned to a soldier nearby.

"Take a few people ahead—make sure there's nothing waiting to ambush us in there."

The woman nodded and left, gathering three people to join her scouting. They came back about ten minutes later, no worse for wear.

"Cave's empty, Sir. There are webs around, but we couldn't see any of those things."

"Good. Get everyone ready to move. The sooner we're in the city, the better. We need a defensible location if we're going to clear the forest."

"Clear...?" I couldn't hold the question back. And now Eleanor saw me, the cold calculation in her eyes replaced by something far more frightening.

Fanaticism.

"We're rebuilding Vijayam from the ground up. A foothold for the empire—an impenetrable fortress."

This wasn't her—wasn't like anything she'd expressed in the past year.

"And what of Ajakava? I thought you didn't want to kill her—or did that also never matter to you?" I asked.

She smiled, the beatific, patronizing smile of the enlightened.

"Ajakava is the one I'm doing this for," she replied. "The visions I saw were what would come to pass if I did not find the city."

That couldn't be it. That didn't match my visions at all. Why would she show us such contrasting dreams?

"Let us go!" Amma cried, struggling against the guard who held her down. "We aren't a threat to you! We're the ones who led you here, aren't we? Why do this now?"

"Because," Eleanor said, kneeling to look into Amma's face, "I can't have your son meddling beyond this point. The scorpion chose us both, but only the first can win. You can all stay tied up here until it's over. I'll leave a few soldiers to keep an eye on you, and then you can go do whatever you want."

Soldiers. She didn't see the blood trickling down Valli's throat where her captor had pressed too close with his blade; didn't see the welt forming on Appa's cheek from the rifle butt that had slammed into it after he was caught.

She didn't see the bloodlust pouring from every other Felter's body.

The moment she left us defenseless in this place, we would be dead.

The others knew it too, I could see the fear growing in them.

Please, I prayed, *save us.*

It began as a trickle; a soft patter on the forest floor that grew quickly into the furious torrent of hundreds of feet closing in on us.

Eleanor wheeled on me, pulled me up by the collar.

"What did you do?" she asked.

"Called for help."

The first spider that broke through the treeline was about the size of a dog, covered in brown hair that sprouted from it like bristles. A gunshot took it between the eyes before it reached the soldiers.

And then the others began leaping from the branches above us, raining terror down on the Felters.

Eleanor didn't wait around. She grabbed a sword from a fallen soldier and ran headlong for the cave. Appa and Amma were the first to give chase, spurred by their desire to kill the god before it awoke.

I rushed after them. I needed to find Ajakava before Eleanor did.

Before any of them did. I had to know her motivations, had to speak with her—for everything she had put me through, I couldn't let them use or kill her before I understood what she wanted with me.

My friends stood transfixed for a moment by the growing number of creatures entering the grove, weaving down on thin lines of string or leaping from tree to tree. Only when the fight began to spill over towards them, in the form of two scorpions turning their sharpened pincers in their direction—all earlier peace forgotten—did they follow.

The beasts let us escape, turning as one instead to attack those with weapons drawn. The spider behind the cave door only waited as long as it took for Bhavani, the last of us to enter, to pass it before it rolled shut the entrance, plunging us into darkness and mercifully cutting short the sounds of the slaughter taking place outside.

"Velu, are you there?" Bhavani asked. I heard her hand slap against the wall and reached out to grasp it.

We found Ravi and Muthu similarly huddled, our group forming itself into small pockets in the void, seeking what minor comforts we could in this place. But the others had pushed far ahead, drawn into a race to be the first to find the legendary beast. The four of us, our hands linked as before, followed carefully, our ears searching for the sound of arachnid feet. We knew they were all around us, but the creatures had gone silent, leaving our ragged breaths the only sounds in the dead air.

"Appa and Amma?" I asked.

"Ran off ahead. Valli too," Ravi said.

We inched our way towards an exit, one hand kept against the web-sticky wall at all times. Tiny creatures crawled over us, so we shut our mouths and pushed ahead, until I felt the ghost of a breeze brush my face from a passage to our right. It grew stronger as we ventured towards it, but there was no light to accompany it. But the cave did end, throwing us up into the open world once more.

A world lit only by the light of a million stars glimmering like diamonds in the midnight sky.

"Why is it dark?" Muthu asked over the wind, which had grown into a gale.

"Where are they?" Bhavani asked.

I turned to look for the cave, but the door-spider had closed the passage behind us. We were trapped here.

"What is this place?" Ravi asked. I followed his gaze, looked to the floor.

We stood in the dried-up remains of a river. The ground now was a carpet of corpses, desiccated and ancient. Those who had tried to flee or fight the fall of Vijayam, who had run into the river seeking passage beyond an ancient waterfall. A litany of failures.

Around us grew the crags of the immense Katalkad, enclosing us in this pit. And in front of us, past this burial ground, was a solitary passage, the lost path to a dead city.

"We can figure out what it is later. For now, we have to find the others," Bhavani said.

The first corpse in front of her crumbled under her feet, its contents long since dissipated—or consumed. We followed suit. Nothing left but to follow the road.

Come to me.

Beyond the valley bottleneck the road widened into a once-grand path now overgrown with weeds and creepers. I could see the road at its height, a memory laid over my present, clogged with bullock carts and travelers of all kinds walking to and from Vijayam with no fear of assault. Shrines and sacrifice tethers marked the road at regular intervals—stations to give thanks to the protector of the forest and her children.

I followed their path to the great gates, the ones I knew so well now. And in Ajakava's memory, the gilded murals were not faded and worn by time but shining, pristine wonders of art.

That showed a city led by its kings bowing to a great beast of obsidian, arms raised in obeisance to their god.

Enter. And you shall see.

The voice was a whisper that sent the wind into a frenzy, making it push all of us past the gates, giving us no time to consider the invitation. It stayed there, formed a wall, a vortex that pushed Ravi back when he tried to touch it.

"You all heard that, didn't you?" Muthu asked.

The others nodded.

"Is that what you've been hearing all this time?" Bhavani asked me.

"It sounds like nails scraping rock," Ravi said, shuddering.

"She's trying to show us the truth," I said. "Did you see the murals on the gate? Appa's story had Ajakava change carapace when it turned evil, but these people worshipped a *black* scorpion."

They looked at one another, confused, concerned.

"Velu, we saw a broken old gate. Nothing was on it."

I growled.

"If you can speak to all of them, then you can show them everything too!" I yelled into the sky.

That is your job.

Ajakava sounded amused now that we were close.

"What is she showing you?" Bhavani asked. "That could help us find her, and Appa."

At least they weren't questioning the visions anymore.

I told them what I had seen on the way into the city, and then I looked beyond the causeway, into the ancient city of Vijayam itself.

I saw the city as it was now, its buildings crumbling, covered in moss and vine, stranglers growing to straddle their walls; drape them in ropes of impenetrable wood. Somewhere beyond them, I knew was the amphitheatre I had visited so many times in my dreams. Then the forest receded, faded even as the stone built itself up, guided by unseen hands. The people returned, as the scorpion showed me a time when it was allowed—welcomed—into the streets of this city.

I saw through her eyes, walked down cobbled pathways flanked by multicolored, vibrant homes. The people bowed to me as I passed, their hands clasped in reverence, their legs steady. No hint of fear. And I felt pride.

We followed the main road, which wound around two great aqueducts—though I paused a moment to revel in the sight of youths playing and laughing in the deep pools. Beyond this, at the city's heart, stood its fort-castle, built upon a hill broken by a god's fist, crumbled into a mound of countless immense rocks. The first king of Vijayam had needed *my* aid in constructing that palace, in clearing enough of the rock for his people to build a palace atop it.

I climbed the winding staircase I had helped build, whose stone I had carried on my back from the mines deep within my mountains. And at the summit, I saw the palace, pearlescent, glowing under my protection. I saw a lineage of kings, an unbroken chain of friendship extending through countless centuries, until the last. Until the one who looked upon me and saw a beast. A threat.

A monster.

Ram.

He glowered at me from under eyes darkened by fatigue, a mind fogged by paranoia.

"Valli!" Muthu's cry broke the vision, jarred me back into our time, where the palace before us was less pearlescent and more the colour of opium-rotted teeth. Its spires lay fallen across its courtyard—once the site of a massive garden, now a mess of weeds, puddles, and pitchers.

Valli sat propped up against one of these spires now, a hand pressed to her thigh, her eyes closed.

"What happened to you?" Muthu asked.

"We chased the white lady from the cave all the way here. Until then she didn't seem to care that we were following." She paused, took a shuddering breath. "But when we got up here, she stopped. Just stood still, like she wasn't in her body anymore. And then she went mad; started swinging at all of us with a dagger. Got me good in the leg—scraped bone. And then she ran off inside somewhere."

She stopped, breathed through clenched teeth again.

"And Appa and Amma?" Bhavani asked.

"Went after her. They weren't hurt."

"Sorry, Valli," I said.

"Go, I'll stay with her," Muthu said.

"Me too. Better we stay out here in case those things around decide to eat us after all," Ravi added.

That left Bhavani and me, and we didn't need to discuss our options.

We checked our weapons, strung our bows, then entered the yawning door of the Vijayam Palace.

* * *

The palace was a shell—a husk of what had been the pinnacle of creation. Appa's story told that King Ram had sealed Ajakava beneath the palace—and that part seemed to hold weight, as evidence of that battle scarred the pillars and walls that still stood. But the floor had fallen in, taking with it the pavilion and thrones that had once stood in this space. The place where Ram and Ajakava were said to have ended their epic battle.

Find me.

I jumped into the pit.

I did not fall as far as I imagined, only a dozen feet and I was on solid ground once more. The scorpion had dug a passage into the bedrock of the hill, made herself a home to recover from her wounds.

And now she was preparing for the second battle for her life.

I lit a torch and took the lead, confirming what my hands and ears had already told me: there were no other beasts in this place. It was the home of a god, and none but her could enter. At the cave's end was a wider cavern, and that was where the god lay.

Her bulk took up half the cavern, filling it with a black mass that blended with the shadows of this place, a carapace of polished onyx larger than my mind could accommodate.

I moved the torch, took in the scorpion's immensity, and that's when I saw her, Eleanor, her white hair wild over her face, which had fallen into an expression of maddened serenity. She stood before the sleeping giant's face as if transfixed.

"Velu! Bhavani!" Amma's call was a hiss coming from a corner of this cavern, behind an outcropping of wall—as much shelter as there was in this place. I glanced back at Eleanor, but she didn't seem to notice; or if she did, she didn't care.

She'd found what she had come for. I had lost.

We joined Appa and Amma in their hiding spot, keeping low and watching Eleanor as she explored the scorpion's body, muttering to herself.

"What is she doing?" Amma asked.

"She's making notes," I said. I had seen her do this before, but usually with a sketch book in her hands. She'd lost hers somewhere on the way here.

"If she touches the beast, I'm shooting," Appa said.

I had to do something now, before he ruined us—like Ram had done Vijayam.

I left the hiding spot, pulling away from Bhavani's grasp, and ventured towards Eleanor and the sleeping god.

She blinked when she saw me, trying to recall who I was. Her face lit up when she did, as if we were observing an interesting tree formation or butterfly, and not standing in front of a god of arachnids who had caused the death of a civilization.

As if she were not actively trying to use that destructive power to conquer my people.

And strangely, I found myself smiling back.

"Velu, did you have any idea she'd be this big?" she asked, grinning like a child at play.

"I knew she was big, but this is...incredible," I replied.

"Isn't it? It is magnificent. A wonder."

"What are you going to do, though? You've lost your sketchbook."

She tapped her skull with one long finger. "It's all up here. I'll never forget this thing, not even if I tried."

And her expression changed, her face slackened, as her hand dropped from her head, reached out to caress the scorpion's pincer.

Appa's arrow came a moment too late, piercing Eleanor's arm just as it touched the god.

Eyes opened. Two large ones atop her head, and five each on either side of her mandibles. Twelve red orbs, frowning in a sleep-fugue.

Eleanor grabbed at the arrow, broke the shaft and cried out in pain. Ajakava paid her no heed. But I couldn't avoid her, couldn't even avert my gaze when those twelve eyes swiveled to focus on me.

You found me.

The god of Vijayam—the scourge of Vijayam—was surprised.

"Velu, get away from her!" Appa cried. I heard the arrow leave his bow, the whistle in the still air as it cut towards Ajakava, only to bounce harmlessly off the scorpion's face.

I did not think you would come.

She showed no sign that she had felt the blow.

"You called me here. You promised me the truth."

I have shown it to you.

"Show it to them!"

"Velu? Are you...speaking with it?" Bhavani asked.

"That is the devil, Velu. Do not heed her whispers," Appa said.

I cannot. They do not want to see it.

"What did you bring me here for, then?" I asked.

Sustenance.

My feet worked now, and I fell onto my back. The scorpion, however, did not move.

A joke. You know what I feed on. Why I have lain dormant for so many years.

The kings bowing to it, the streets of people safe and reverent. A bond through ages, broken by fearful arrogance.

What else would a god of protection feed on but the happiness of her worshippers?

"Why isn't it attacking?" Amma whispered.

"You want purpose," I said.

Yes.

Ajakava's voice shuddered in my mind, the cobwebs dusted free of her brain. A god finding herself once more.

"Why won't you speak to me? I was the one who found you!" Eleanor cried. Her hand was wrapped around her wound, though it also seemed to have shocked her back into a semblance of sanity.

Ajakava turned the power of her gaze onto Eleanor and must have spoken to her from the way her body stiffened, the way her grip tightened around the hole in her arm.

She paled further, and when the god's eyes left her, Eleanor Greyback fled from her home.

"What did you show her?" I asked.

I gave her an opportunity, and a warning.

She would say no more.

Bhavani pulled free of Appa's grip now and joined me; faced the scorpion.

"What do you mean, she wants purpose?" she asked, still eyeing Ajakava nervously.

"Appa's story has it twisted; a legend based on a lie. Ajakava was not the one to turn on the city, to grow greedy for power. It was Ram who was afraid of her, whose paranoia drove him to attack the god who protected his people."

"God. Not demon."

Ajakava, the Forest Guardian.

Bhavani's eyes widened, and I knew the voice had reached her too.

Amma seemed conflicted, caught between us and Appa, who was still shaking his head— his right hand still hovering at his quiver.

"Think about it, Appa," I said. "She *led* us here, never once did her children attack us."

"They attacked Eleanor's group from the outset, but never once harmed us," Bhavani said.

He was wavering now.

"We are all descendants of the forest. Everyone but the Felters," Amma said. She understood.

"Invaders. *Threats.*"

A purpose for the awakened god.

This is not their home.

Appa heard it now, but he shook his head still.

"This thing killed your friend! Or have you both forgotten that?" he asked.

My control of my children...was weak. They are predators, and their instincts during my convalescence have sometimes been stronger than my commands. I am sorry.

"And if we all pray to you, it won't happen again? Give ourselves up to you, or your children will eat us? Some protection, that."

This was a test. Appa was testing the conviction of a *god*.

I do not want your faith—only your safety. Now that I have awoken, this will not happen again.

Appa thought about this a moment, his eyes never leaving Ajakava's main pair.

"And if we believe your story, then what? You'll kill all the Felters? And when they come back with a hundred frigates, then what? Spiders and scorpions cannot defeat guns and artillery!"

"Ships cannot enter the forest," I said.

"And the forest protects its own," Amma added. Appa's hand fell from the quiver, defeated.

Ajakava hummed in our heads, sibilant; happy.

"What do we do now?" Appa asked.

"Go back, get ready to fight," Bhavani guessed.

Return to the surface.

This was a command now, delivered with a thrum of power that insisted I follow it.

"And you?" I asked.

I will follow. I must gather my strength.

"We can't do anything in this fight." I realized. "We're going first to save everyone."

Again, the command came. And this time, we followed. Appa and Amma went first, followed by Bhavani, then me. I turned back once to look at the scorpion, but I could no longer see her in the gloom.

We climbed out of the pit and found the others close to where we left them, if somewhat more on edge.

"What happened down there?" Ravi asked. "The Felter lady ran past not long ago, straight into the forest."

We filled them in. They were skeptical, and it took Appa's resigned nod to convince them of our tale.

"So, she's going to be waiting for us in the city with all her people ready to fight?" Ravi asked.

"If they believe her," I said.

"And what of Guna? How does her family fit into this story?" Valli asked. "Whatever this god told you, her creatures still killed some of ours."

"We knew the forest was dangerous. *We* knew to avoid it. The scorpion wasn't what forced them into the forest. She wasn't what coerced them, made it an expedition they convinced themselves was an opportunity," I said.

"We know not to blame the leopard or the crocodile if they kill one of ours. How is this any different?" Bhavani asked.

They were silent, and stayed sullenly so as we returned through the ruins and the valley cave to the forest we knew, where the sun still shone through small gaps in the canopy.

We did not stay long at the battle that had taken place there, though little remained but backpacks and dried blood and arachnid corpses.

Of Eleanor, there was no sign.

Our journey back to Vallarpattinam was quiet, our earlier guides having retreated out of sight. Conversation was scarce, each of us coming to terms with everything we'd seen, everything we'd learned, and preparing ourselves for what was to come.

We did not know what was to come in the town, but we knew that it would not be easy.

We knew that we might not all make it through to the other side.

* * *

It took us three days to reach our homes on the town's outskirts. We spent the day traveling through Vallarpattinam, telling everyone there to leave, or to stay indoors for a few days. Eleanor, presumably, was doing the same within the Town. We had barely covered half the town when the first horns sounded from the fort, signaling the advent of Ajakava's army.

The god breached first, a dark mass that broke through the tree line. She waited there, one pincer raised, as her horde pooled around her. A teeming mass of insects, arachnids and beasts of the forest that swarmed to the Protector's call.

They were legion.

There was movement now at the Felt Town walls as their garrison hurried to move cannons and archers and musketeers into position. They had not heeded Eleanor's warnings, then.

But for every creature felled by their cannonballs, there were a dozen to take their place.

We rushed everyone we could indoors, cleared as many of the streets as we could, before Ajakava's pincer fell, and the forest began its march.

There was nothing more we could do. Nothing to mitigate what was coming. We didn't even have the time to hide ourselves now, and so we waited together, next to Appa's house, and waited to be overrun.

They hit Vallarpattinam with the force of a cyclone, rattling homes with the force of their steps. They climbed overhead and crawled underfoot—a wave of exoskeleton and flesh coming to scour the earth. But then it passed, as quickly as it had begun, the army moving to begin its true assault—on the walls of Felt Town. Our town had the look of a storm's aftermath, but as the people began peering out of their homes, we learned one thing:

Ajakava had kept her promise.

The god herself stayed outside the city, observing now, rather than participating in the slaughter she had deemed necessary.

And then the Felters turned their cannonballs upon the town. Their guns roared in their panicked attempts at fending off the assault, but more balls tore into the streets and homes of our town than hit the beasts, who continued undaunted.

Cries of pain echoed through Vallarpattinam now, a final indictment of these occupiers, these invaders. A final toll sealing their fates here.

They did not care that they killed us in their fear. Collateral damage, acceptable losses—if it meant that their kind were saved by it. Sacrifices.

And the forest took note.

And the forest responded.

The god descended upon them.

* * *

I made my choice early, when I saw what remained of one of those unfortunate enough to be struck by a cannon. And nearby, Appa and Bhavani akka had made the same choice.

"Go, we'll get the wounded out of danger," Amma said, waving over to Ravi and Muthu, who were ushering more people into the house they'd stashed Valli in.

I pulled my bow from my back and strung it, and then we walked, unmolested, into Felt Town.

There were civilians within the town— noncombatants, children, servants and guards who worked for the invaders—who should not be subject to Ajakava's wrath. We knew already that there was little we could do to help the horde, not that they required any. And so, we took it upon ourselves to ensure that they were pointed in the right direction.

The streets just within the walls were abandoned, with little stirring within them. We approached with caution, though the only sounds we could hear were of far-off combat, somewhere near the harbor. Already Ajakava's army had forced the Felters back.

"Keep an eye out for broken doors—see where the beasts might have forced their way into houses," Appa said.

"What if the Felters attack us?" Bhavani asked.

"If they're soldiers, kill them. The others are not to be harmed," he replied.

Appa's voice carried the steel of one who's done this before—who knows the cost war carries, and who has come to terms with it. If driving them away required force, required us to become killers, then so be it.

We stayed together, going door-to-door through the streets of Felt Town. Most lay open, a trail of discarded belongings tracing a path from the houses all the way to the harbor. They had evacuated the town when the forest army had shown itself.

Soon, we began coming across the bodies, the first signs of combat within these walls. The very first was of a spider, its body riddled through with bullets. More of the creatures' bodies stained the cobbled roads beyond there, the vanguard suffering the first few volleys of gunfire before those behind them broke the lines.

Even the battle-hardened militia and privateers of Merino hadn't lasted long once that had happened. There was only so much courage a man could muster in the face of nightmares, and this foe was beyond their imagination. Many lay cut down where they tried to flee, puncture wounds in their backs where spider mandibles or scorpion stingers had pierced them. And there, once the fighting grew thick, the leaders of this colony acted in desperation. They began their bombardment. The cobbled path had become a field of impact craters and stray limbs, tearing through soldier and arachnid alike. Anything that had been too slow to get out of their path had been destroyed.

The smell made me want to retch, and I saw Bhavani akka stifle the same urge next to me. Appa, however, was unfazed.

"Don't look away, Velu. This is what you wanted," he said. "This is what it takes, to reclaim this land."

"I want them to leave; not for them to be slaughtered to a man!" I protested.

"It's too late for that now, with what we've unleashed."

"That can't be true," Bhavani said, turning to me. "You've spoken to the thing. Can you stop it?"

I nodded, not trusting to open my mouth without throwing up.

"Then let's go. Appa, you continue searching for survivors," Bhavani said, dragging me away before Appa or I could protest.

For his part, Appa simply pursed his lips and watched us until we turned out of his sight, with a deep sadness shadowing his face.

"Quickly, Velu," Bhavani said. "They won't last much longer, I feel."

We ran through the ever-increasing carnage of Felt Town, trying not to look at the mangled corpses littering the street and wondering who they were—if we had ever sold meat to them or spoken with them. That body there, the one holding a hoe: was that Eleanor's stable hand? The other one there, wasn't that one of the soldiers who had accosted me some weeks ago?

I tried not to let the thoughts settle, shook my head to drive them out, but that only served to root them deeper within me.

I had killed them.

Me, as much as Ajakava or her children. I had found her, woken her to this purpose. I wanted this to happen, just like Appa said. They had died because of me, as if I had drawn my bow and shot them down myself.

And I had seen enough. Our purpose was achieved. More than this would make us—Ajakava and me both—monsters.

We ran for the harbour, following the sounds of gunfire and screaming. The town's outer wall had been torn apart by the cannons, leaving its surroundings strewn with rubble. Beyond, the town's defenders—soldiers and militia alike—fought desperately against their foes, holding them off until every civilian had boarded the boats that would be their salvation. Offshore, a crowd formed at the deck of each Felter ship, anxiously watching the fight.

And observing this all from atop the ruined wall, was the gleaming black shape of the god herself.

They are strong. But that strength made them overconfident, lax. They did not believe anything could challenge them.

Blood glistened at the edges of the sharp pincers, evidence of her having taken part in the fight. A new dent showed in her carapace, where a cannon gunner must have attempted to stop her in her tracks. But now she did not fight, she simply watched as the Felters were pushed further back down the pier, closer and closer to the water.

The last of the boats had left with civilians, leaving only a few dozen soldiers to sacrifice themselves.

The battle was over. It had lasted less than three hours.

From here, I could see their faces, pale and terrified. They bared weapons at the beasts that closed in on them, but their hands quivered, and tears spotted their cheeks. And I realized just how young all of them were. No older than me, at the worst.

"This is enough," I said.

Ajakava turned the weight of her gaze onto me.

They are the enemy.

"They are children! Far too young to be fighting, and far too young to be dying in a foreign land at the hands of creatures they have only seen before in their nightmares!" I yelled. I faced her in full, holding her gaze, refusing to bow to the pressure they inflicted.

And I saw in her alien visage confusion. She did not know how to deal with this.

"You claimed not to be a monster. You claimed that history has twisted your image, made you far worse than you were. But if you kill these people now, what will those who have fled think of you? What do you think they see when they look at you?"

She clicked her pincers in annoyance. She really did not like being called a monster.

What would you have me do, then? she asked, reluctantly.

"Pull your children back into the town, leave the survivors on the beach, let their fellows come for them. And let them all leave."

And if they see this for weakness and attack?

"Then you may do whatever you please. But I beg you, do not become that which you abhor."

The pincers clicked again, and as they did, the forest's army stepped away, turning their backs on their helpless victims and returning as one to the ruins of Felt Town. Confusion turned quickly to a panicked cry for rescue, the soldiers wasting little time to make use of this improbable avenue of escape. I stayed with Ajakava as three boats returned at pace, watching as the soldiers scrambled and fell onboard before they took off with similar haste.

The battle was over. We had won.

The beasts left, returning to the forest now that their work was done, their summons complete. Only the god herself remained with me, peering from the edge of the docks out at the Felter ships that had managed to escape to open water. And a sudden doubt struck me.

"What if they return with more ships, more armies?"

If she does what she is meant to, then they will not.

She?

I peered out, craning to see as much as I could. And I could barely tell from this distance, but I thought I saw a white-haired figure leaning against the gunwale of one, staring back at us.

"So, she escaped," I said.

A knot loosened somewhere within me; my shoulders relaxed; my jaw unclenched. I was *relieved*. I didn't believe that she deserved to die, and more than that—we had been co-conspirators, the first to believe in this god, the ones who had stirred her back to life. I had considered her a friend, until the end.

And for her sake, I hoped she would never return.

I gave her the chance to stay.

"What?"

A chance to learn all she wanted—once I had purged this infestation.

More tests.

"She chose well, then."

I expected nothing less from my champions.

We watched until her frigate's mainsail disappeared beyond the horizon, and I bid Eleanor a silent, final farewell. Hopefully her next expedition would end better than this one had.

And as I watched the people of Vallarpattinam filter into Felt Town to gaze upon their god, I found myself calm. I breathed deeply of the sea air, turned my head skyward.

What now?

"This wasn't the only town the invaders took."

Show me.

And so, we went to find a map.

ACKNOWLEDGEMENTS

I'd like to thank my wife, Anjali, for being my critic and supporter through many, many years. I'd also like to thank my parents and sister for their unwavering faith in me. And finally, I want to thank my writing group of Prashanth, Pritesh, Lavanya, Gautam, and Amal, without whose help (and dedication to their craft), I wouldn't have finished a single story.

ABOUT THE AUTHOR

Chaitanya Murali is a fantasy author who lives in Bangalore, India. When he isn't writing, he's either playing games or watching sports. His work has appeared in *Podcastle Magazine*, *Mithila Review*, *Mythaxis Magazine*, *The Common Tongue Magazine*, and is forthcoming in *Kaleidotrope*. He can be found on Twitter or Instagram @chaitanyamurali.

Please take a moment to review this book at your favorite retailer's website, Goodreads, or simply tell your friends!